Parents and Caregivers,

Stone Arch Readers are designed to provide enjoyable reading experiences, as well as opportunities to develop vocabulary, literacy skills, and comprehension. Here are a few ways to support your beginning reader:

- Talk with your child about the ideas addressed in the story.

- Discuss each illustration, mentioning the characters, where they are, and what they are doing.

- Read with expression, pointing to each word. You may want to read the whole story through and then revisit parts of the story to ensure that the meanings of words or phrases are understood.

- Talk about why the character did what he or she did and what your child would do in that situation.

- Help your child connect with characters and events in the story.

Remember, reading with your child should be fun, not forced. Each moment spent reading with your child is a priceless investment in his or her literacy life.

Gail Saunders-Smith, Ph.D.

STONE ARCH READERS

are published by Stone Arch Books, a Capstone Imprint
1710 Roe Crest Drive
North Mankato, Minnesota 56003
www.capstonepub.com

Library of Congress Cataloging-in-Publication Data
Klein, Adria F. (Adria Fay), 1947-
Freight Train / by Adria Klein ; illustrated by Craig Cameron.
p. cm. -- (Stone Arch readers: Train time)
Summary: Freight Train waits patiently while his cars
are filled with cargo to carry.
ISBN 978-1-4342-4190-0 (library binding)
ISBN 978-1-4342-4885-5 (pbk.)
1. Railroad trains--Juvenile fiction. [1. Railroad trains--
Fiction.] I. Cameron, Craig, ill. II. Title.
PZ7.K678324Fre 2013
[E]--dc23
2012026290

Reading Consultants:
Gail Saunders-Smith, Ph.D.
Melinda Melton Crow, M.Ed.
Laurie K. Holland, Media Specialist
Designer: Russell Griesmer

Printed in the United States of America in Stevens Point, Wisconsin.
092012   006937WZS13

Freight
Train

written by
Adria F. Klein

illustrated by
Craig Cameron

STONE ARCH BOOKS
a capstone imprint

Freight Train was big.

But Freight Train was empty.

"I have nothing to carry,"
he said.

It was time to fill Freight Train.

There were bananas.

13

There were tomatoes.

There were potatoes.

There were oranges.

There were apples.

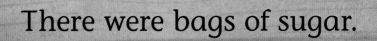

There were bags of sugar.

There were bags of flour.

"Now I am full,"
Freight Train said.

"Time to go!" he said.

Toot! Toot!

STORY WORDS

freight   empty   full

train   carry

Word Count: 62